April Fool's Surprise

Double Trouble

Ready, Freddy!

Double Trouble

April Fool's Surprise

by ABBY KLEIN

illustrated by
JOHN McKINLEY

Scholastic Inc.

New York Toronto London Auckland
Sydney Mexico City New Delhi Hong Kong

To Gigi and Nicky—
Two super cool twins!
Love,
A.K.

No part of this publication may be reproduced, stored in a retrieval
system, or transmitted in any form or by any means, electronic,
mechanical, photocopying, recording, or otherwise, without written
permission of the publisher. For information regarding permission,
write to Scholastic Inc., Attention: Permissions Department,
557 Broadway, New York, NY 10012.

ISBN 978-0-545-29495-9

Text copyright © 2012 by Abby Klein
Illustrations copyright © 2012 by John McKinley
All rights reserved. Published by Scholastic Inc.
SCHOLASTIC and associated logos are trademarks
and/or registered trademarks of Scholastic Inc.

12 11 10 9 8 7 6 5 4 3 2 1   12 13 14 15 16 17/0

Printed in the U.S.A.   40
First printing, February 2012

CHAPTERS

My name is Kasey, and I have a twin
sister named Kelly. Whenever we're
together, crazy things happen.
That's why everyone calls us
Double Trouble.

One time on April Fool's Day,
we got into a little trouble.

Let me tell you about it.

CHAPTER 1

Mike, Ike, and Rocky

"Mom! Mom!" I called. "Kelly and I are going over to Jake's for a little bit."

"Hang on a minute," our mom called back. She came jogging into the kitchen with our little brother, Kenny, in her arms. Our two wiener dogs, Mike and Ike, came running in behind her. "Would you please take Mike and Ike with you? They really need to go for a walk."

Mike and Ike barked and started running in circles.

"But Jake lives right next door," I said. "That's not much of a walk."

"I'm sure Rocky needs to get outside, too," said my mom. "You could all take a little walk around the neighborhood."

"Okeydokey," said Kelly.

Kenny clapped his hands and said, "Walk! Walk!"

"Not you, Mister Sillypants," said our mom. "You're staying here with me."

Kenny frowned and stuck out his lower lip.

I kissed him on the cheek. "Maybe later, bud," I said.

Kelly and I grabbed the leashes, put them on the dogs, and ran out. About three seconds later, we were knocking on Jake's back door.

His dog, Rocky, started barking and jumping around like crazy inside the house. Rocky loves

Mike and Ike even though he's about three times as big as they are.

Jake yelled through the door, "Hey, guys, what's up?"

"Want to go for a walk?" we yelled back.

"Just a second," said Jake. "I just have to get Rocky's leash on."

"Good luck with that," Kelly said, giggling. Rocky was so excited that he wouldn't sit still for a second. He kept popping up and down like a jumping bean.

"If you just let me get this leash on, then you can go out," Jake said.

I peeked through the window.

"What's going on in there?" asked Kelly.

"It looks like a wrestling match, but I couldn't tell you who was winning."

Mike and Ike were wagging their tails and whimpering.

"It shouldn't be too much longer," I said.

"I don't know about that," said Kelly. "That dog is cra-zy!"

Finally Jake got the leash on, and they came bursting through the door. Rocky almost stepped on Mike and Ike as he bounded out of the house.

"Whoa! Whoa! Hang on there, buddy," Jake yelled, as he tried to grab a better hold of the leash.

I laughed. "I think Rocky is taking you for a walk," I said.

"He'll calm down in a minute," Jake called over his shoulder, as Rocky dragged him across the front lawn. "He just gets very excited about his walks."

"You can say that again," said Kelly.

We raced to catch up. Mike and Ike may be small, but they're super fast on their short little legs.

"So, what's up?" asked Jake.

"Tomorrow's the big day," said Kelly.

"Yeah," I said. "We need your help."

"I'm not very good at math," said Jake. "I don't really think I can help you."

"We're not talking about the math test, ding-dong," I said.

"You're not?"

"No," said Kelly.

"Then what are you talking about?" asked Jake.

"What day is it today?" I said.

"March thirty-first," said Jake.

"So that means tomorrow is . . . ?"

"April first," said Jake.

"And that is . . . ?" said Kelly.

Just then, Rocky yanked on the leash. Jake tripped and fell right into a big puddle of mud.

He looked up at us and said, "April Fool's Day!" Mud dripped off his hair onto his face.

Kelly and I burst out laughing. "Looks like Rocky played his trick on you a day early."

Jake stood up. He was muddy from head to toe.

We couldn't stop laughing.

"What's so funny?"

"You look like a huge chocolate monster," we said.

"I can't believe I almost forgot that tomorrow is April Fool's Day," said Jake. "It's, like, my favorite day of the year!"

"We know," Kelly said. "That's why we need your help. You always come up with great tricks to play on people."

"Yeah, we want to play some really good tricks on people this year," I said.

"Well, I've got some really good ones," said Jake.

"Tell us! Tell us!" we said.

"I found a website where kids posted their favorite April Fool's Day tricks," said Jake. "I actually made a list of the best ones."

"Cool," said Kelly.

"Awesome," I said. "Will you share them with us?"

"Of course," said Jake. "I have the list in my room."

"Let's go now!" said Kelly.

"First I think I need to change out of these

muddy, wet clothes," said Jake. "I don't think your mom wants a swamp monster walking through her house."

I laughed. "Good idea," I said.

"Why don't you guys take Mike and Ike home, and I'll meet you at your house with the list in about ten minutes."

"Okeydokey," said Kelly.

"See you in about ten minutes," I said.

Rocky saw a squirrel and took off like a rocket, with Jake racing behind.

"Don't forget the list!" I called after him.

CHAPTER 2

The List

Jake took Rocky home, changed out of his muddy clothes, and arrived at our house a few minutes later.

As usual, he walked right in the back door without even knocking. "Hi, Mrs. Thresher," said Jake.

"Oh, hi, Jake," said our mom.

"Jake! Jake!" Kenny said, waddling over to him.

"Hey, big guy," said Jake. "Give me five."

Jake lifted up Kenny's plump little hand and gave it a gentle slap. Kenny laughed.

"I didn't know you were coming over," said our mom.

Jake held up the list. "Yeah, Kasey, Kelly, and I have something we have to work on."

"Really? What is it?" asked our mom.

I looked at Jake. Jake looked at Kelly. Kelly looked at me.

"Uh, nothing," said Jake.

"Jake's just helping us with something for our math test tomorrow," Kelly said.

"Good one," I whispered to Kelly.

"That's nice of you," said our mom.

"No problem," said Jake.

"So we'll be up in our room if you need us, Mom," I said.

"Me go! Me go!" said Kenny.

"Sorry, but you can't go," Mom said. "They have some important studying to do. Maybe they can play with you when they're done."

Our mom scooped up Kenny in her arms. "How about you and I go fold the laundry?" They walked out of the room.

"That sounds like a blast," Jake said.

"It is for Kenny," Kelly said. "He plays in the laundry basket while my mom does the folding."

"Come on," I said. "Let's go upstairs. I can't wait to see that list."

We climbed the stairs to our room and opened the door. Pete, our gecko, ran right up Jake's pant leg.

"Hey there, Pete," Jake said. "How ya doing today?" He patted him on the back. Pete crawled up Jake's stomach and sat on his shoulder. "Do you want to see our secret list, Pete?"

"I do," I said.

"Me, too," said Kelly.

"How about if I read the ideas to you, and you tell me the ones you like," said Jake.

"Okay," we said together.

"Listen to this one. You tie a rubber band
around the handle to the sprayer hose on
your sink. Then when your mom turns on
the water in the morning, she gets sprayed in
the face."

"Ha, ha, ha! That's hilarious!" Kelly said.

"We are definitely doing that one," I said.

"What other ideas do you have?" said Kelly.

"Here's another good one," said Jake. "You add a few drops of green food coloring to someone's milk. Then when that person takes a sip, she freaks out because she thinks she just drank spoiled milk."

"We should play that trick on Madison at school tomorrow," Kelly said.

"Yeah," I said. "She would definitely freak out."

"How are you going to get the food coloring into her milk?" asked Jake.

"Easy," I said. "She always drinks milk at snack time. You can distract her while we put the drops in."

"Great plan!" said Jake. "I can't wait to see her face."

"Me, either," said Kelly.

"You guys should bring the food coloring,"

said Jake. "I don't even know if my mom has any."

"We definitely have some in the cupboard," I said. "It's left over from Saint Patrick's Day, when we made green cupcakes for the leprechauns."

"We'll bring it for sure," said Kelly.

"Here's a good trick to play on your dad," said Jake. "You take the salt out of the salt shaker and put sugar in instead. Then when your dad goes to put salt on his eggs, he's actually putting sugar all over them. When he takes a bite of his breakfast, he'll want to spit it out because it'll taste so gross!"

"Awesome!" said Kelly. "We have to do that one, sis."

"Ha, ha, ha!" Jake laughed.

"What's so funny?" we asked.

"This next one would be great to do on Kenny."

"Really?" I said. "What is it?"

"You draw a mustache on his face while he's sleeping."

"We did draw on our cousin's face last Christmas," Kelly said, laughing.

"And this time we can use washable marker," I said. "That way Mom and Dad can't get too mad at us!"

"If you do that one, make sure you take a picture," said Jake. "I have to see little Kenny with a mustache."

"Got any more ideas?" asked Kelly. "These are all so great."

"Well, I do have one more," said Jake, smiling, "but it's not on this list."

"Really? What is it?" I asked.

"I think it's the best trick of all," said Jake.

"Tell us! Tell us!" we said.

"I think the best April Fool's Day trick of all would be for the two of you to switch places at school tomorrow."

Kelly and I looked at each other.

"You both pretend to be the other person for the day. See how long it takes for Mr. Lopez to notice."

"Oh, he'll recognize us right away," I said.

"Oh, no he won't. You two look exactly alike.

I can tell you apart because we've known each other since we were babies, but most people can't tell the difference between the two of you."

"But Mr. Lopez always calls us by the right name," said Kelly.

"That's because you always wear a skirt and put your hair in a ponytail, and Kasey always wears jeans and puts her hair in braids."

"Really?"

"Really," said Jake. "If you two switched your clothes and hair tomorrow, then I really think it could work."

"That would be such a great trick if we could pull it off," I said. "Want to do it, sis?"

"Yes, I do!" said Kelly.

"That's the best idea ever!" we said, hugging Jake. "You're a genius!"

"Great! Then I'll see the two of you tomorrow," Jake said, as he started to leave. "And don't tell anyone," he whispered.

"We won't!"

I looked at Kelly, and she looked at me. "It'll just be our little secret," I said.

"Yep," said Kelly. Then she winked at me and smiled. "Our little secret."

CHAPTER 3

Spaghetti Head

"Girls, wash your hands. Dinner is in ten minutes!" our mom called from downstairs.

"Already?" I said.

"I can't believe it," said Kelly. "We have so much to do to get ready for tomorrow."

"I know," I said. "How about we make a list of the things we need?"

"I could," Kelly said, laughing, "if Harry wasn't sitting on the notepad."

Harry is our pet tarantula. I picked him up

off the notepad and put him on my head. That's one of his favorite places to sit.

"Okay," said Kelly, "ready."

"Well," I said, "we need a rubber band."

"Don't we have a nice big one on our slingshot?" asked Kelly.

"Yes, we do," I said, smiling. "That one will be perfect."

"We need to find the washable markers to draw the mustache on Kenny's face," said Kelly.

"I think the last time we used them was when we drew hearts on Honey Buns for Valentine's Day."

"Oh yeah," said Kelly, laughing. "I almost forgot about that."

"We need the sugar and the green food coloring."

"Dinnertime!" yelled Mom.

"Let's go down and eat," Kelly said, "and then maybe we can do some stuff when Mom is giving Kenny his bath."

"Good thinking," I said. We gave each other a high five, and I started to run out of the room. Kelly grabbed my shirt and pulled me back in.

"What?"

Kelly pointed to my head. "You know Mom doesn't like any pets at the table."

"I forgot he was up there. Come on, Harry," I said. "Why don't you take a little nap on my pillow while I eat." I gently put him down on my bed.

Kelly and I raced to the stairs and slid down the banister.

Unfortunately, right at that moment our mom had left the kitchen to look for us and saw what we did.

"Girls! How many times have I told you not to slide down the stair railing? It is a very dangerous thing to do!"

"But Mr. Fluffy does it all the time," I said.

"Mr. Fluffy is a cat," said our mom. "You are not a cat!"

"Sorry, Mom," we said.

"Now come on. Dinner is getting cold."

When we walked into the kitchen, Kenny was banging his spoon on his high chair and chanting, "Getti! Getti! Getti!"

"I guess he's hungry," I said.

"Guess so," said our dad.

Mom put a big bowl of spaghetti and meatballs on the table.

"Well, spaghetti and meatballs is his favorite thing to eat," said Kelly.

"Mine, too," I said.

"It won't be tomorrow," Kelly whispered to me, "when we switch places."

I smiled.

"What are you two girls whispering about?" asked our dad.

"Nothing," we said.

"'Nothing' usually means you're up to something," said our mom.

Kenny started to bang his spoon louder. "Eat! Eat! Eat!" he yelled.

"Calm down, little man," said Dad. "It's coming."

Our mom put some cut-up spaghetti into a bowl for Kenny and set it down on his tray. He scooped up a big spoonful and shoved it in his mouth.

"Slow down there, boo-bear," said Kelly, laughing.

"So, your mom tells me that Jake was helping you study for your math test," said our dad.

Kelly and I looked at each other. "Yep," we said.

"Do you need any more help tonight?" asked our dad.

"No, I think we're all set," said Kelly.

"We have some other important work to do tonight," I said.

"I'm glad to see you girls taking your homework so seriously," said Mom.

We smiled.

"Besides the math test, what else is happening at school tomorrow?" asked our dad.

"Just the same old stuff," Kelly said.

"Well, there is one thing . . . ," I said.

Kelly stared at me.

"We're doing a science experiment with food coloring, and Mr. Lopez asked us to bring some in. I think we have some green food coloring. Don't we, Mom?"

"We sure do. It's in the cupboard right next to the sink. You're welcome to bring it to school tomorrow."

"Thanks, Mom," I said.

"In fact, I'll get it down for you right now, so you don't forget it."

Mom got up to get the food coloring. Kelly squeezed my leg under the table.

Kenny started banging on his tray again and shouting, "More! More! More!"

"My goodness!" said our mom. "You finished your whole bowl already! I'll be right there to give you some more."

"That's my boy," said our dad. "He wants to grow up to be big and strong."

Mom brought the food coloring to the table. "Here you go, honey," she said, handing it to me.

"And here you go, little piggie," she said to

Kenny, as she scooped some more spaghetti into his bowl.

This time, instead of eating the spaghetti, Kenny picked up the bowl, and before anyone could stop him, dumped the whole thing on his head.

He sat in his high chair, giggling, with spaghetti noodles in his hair and sauce dripping down his face.

Kelly and I burst out laughing.

"Girls! Stop laughing! It's not funny," said our mom.

"Yes, it is!" we said. "It's hilarious!"

Mom ran over to Kenny and tried to pick some of the noodles out of his hair and wipe the sauce off his face. "Ugh! This is such a mess! I'm going to have to take you straight to the tub, mister, and give you a bath right now."

"I'll help you," said our dad. "I have a feeling this is going to be a big job."

They took Kenny and went upstairs to the bathroom.

"Perfect," I said to Kelly. "Now we have plenty of time to get everything ready."

CHAPTER 4

The Big Salt Switch

"Kelly, go check and see if they're in the bathroom yet," I said.

"Okeydokey!" said Kelly. She tiptoed into the other room and then came racing back. "I can hear the water running, so I think we're safe. Should I go get that rubber band?"

"No, no. We can't do that until after mom has finished doing the dinner dishes. We'll have to sneak downstairs after everyone goes to sleep."

"Oh, good plan," said Kelly.

"Let's see. First, we need to do the old switcheroo with the salt shaker. Go get it and dump out all the salt."

Kelly grabbed the salt shaker from the table and tried to unscrew the cap. "Boy oh boy, this is really tight," she said.

"Here. Give it to me, wimp. Let me try," I said, reaching for the shaker.

Kelly handed it to me, and I tried to get the cap loose. "You're not kidding! It's like someone glued it on," I said. I kept twisting with all my might. "Wait, wait . . . I think it's getting looser."

All of a sudden the cap came flying off, and salt spilled all over the floor.

Kelly picked some up and threw it in the air. "Look! It's snowing!"

"Shhhhh! Stop fooling around," I said. "Help me get this cleaned up. We don't have a lot of time."

We grabbed a couple of sponges and wiped up the floor.

"Now for the sugar."

"There's only one problem," said Kelly.

"What's that?"

"Mom keeps it in that cupboard way up there," Kelly said, pointing to one of the highest cupboards in the kitchen.

"No problem," I said. "We can just stand on a chair."

Kelly started to push a chair across the floor. "Hey, hey, hey, pick it up," I said. "You're making too much noise."

Kelly carried the chair over to the cupboard and climbed on top of it. "Shoot," she said. "I can't reach it."

"Stand on your tippy-toes," I said.

Kelly tried again, but she still couldn't reach. "Now what?"

"I have an idea," I said. "I'll get on my hands

and knees on the chair, and you can stand on my back."

"You're so smart," said Kelly.

"Hop down a minute, so I can get up." I climbed onto the chair and got on my hands and knees. "Now, take your time getting up. Hold on to the counter when you climb on my back."

Kelly slowly climbed up and stood on my back. "Hey, this is kind of like the tricks we do on the balance beam in gymnastics."

"Just get the sugar," I said.

Kelly grabbed the bag of sugar. "Got it!" she said. She put it on the counter and slowly climbed down off my back.

I smiled. "We make a great team," I said.

Kelly held the salt shaker while I poured in the sugar. "Hold it steady," I said.

"Now we just have to put the sugar back, so Mom doesn't suspect anything," said Kelly.

We performed our acrobatics once more and safely put the sugar back where we found it. Then we put the chair away.

"This is going to be great!" said Kelly.

"I know," I said. "I can't wait to see Dad's face when he tastes sugary eggs!"

Just then our dad walked back into the kitchen. "What did you say?" he asked.

"Ummm . . . ummm . . . ," Kelly said.

"I thought I just heard you say 'Dad,'" he said.

Kelly and I looked at each other.

"Kelly was just wondering what was taking so long," I said.

"Yeah, yeah," said Kelly. "I just said to Kasey, 'Where's Dad?'"

"Well, your brother was such a mess. It took forever to get all of those noodles out of his hair. Good thing I was there to help your mother."

"Yeah. Good thing," I said.

"Well, Kasey and I have to finish the rest of our work," Kelly said. "We'll be upstairs if you need us."

I grabbed the green food coloring, and we went upstairs to our room. Harry was still sitting on my pillow. "Hey there, Harry. Did you have a nice nap?"

"Oh, great!" said Kelly.

"What?"

"Skippy got out of his cage. I hope he didn't get caught behind the bookcase again."

We started to search our room for Skippy the hamster. "We need to find him fast, before Mike and Ike do!" I said.

Kelly looked behind the bookcase. "He's not here."

I looked in our beds. "He's not here, either."

"Maybe he's curled up in your robot slippers," said Kelly.

I looked in my slippers. "Nope. Why don't we check under the beds?"

Kelly looked under her bed, and I looked under mine.

"Found him!" Kelly said.

"And look what I found," I said, holding up a pack of markers. "The washable markers! Just what we need for our April Fool's Day trick on Kenny."

There was a knock on our door. We froze.

"Oh no! I hope they didn't hear us!" I whispered.

"Come in!" said Kelly.

"Kenny is going to bed," said our mom. "He wants to say good night."

"Night, night, bud," I said, giving him a kiss.

"Night, night, boo-bear," Kelly said, kissing his other cheek.

"Night, night," Kenny repeated, blowing us kisses.

"Sweet dreams."

"Girls, you have about an hour before you have to get ready for bed."

"Okeydokey," said Kelly.

My mom closed the door. We waited until her footsteps disappeared down the hall before we started talking again.

For the next hour, Kelly and I continued planning for our big day. We practiced drawing mustaches on some paper until we knew just the one we wanted to draw on Kenny. We found the big rubber band we needed for the sink trick. We talked about how we would get the green food coloring into Madison's milk. Kelly picked out an outfit for me, and I picked out an outfit for her in preparation for the big twin switch.

"Girls! Time to get ready for bed," our dad called.

"Already?" said Kelly.

"Time sure flies when you're having fun," I said.

We got ready for bed and our parents tucked us in. "Sleep tight," they said. "Don't let the bed bugs bite."

"Night," we said.

We stayed awake until the house was quiet, and it was really dark.

"Kelly," I whispered, "I think they're asleep."

Kelly sat up in bed. "I think you're right. I don't hear a sound."

"Then it's time for our Secret Mission," I said. "Come on!"

CHAPTER 5

The Secret Mission

"What do you want to do first?" asked Kelly.

"I think we should go downstairs and put the rubber band on the sink hose."

"I've got it right here," said Kelly, as she pulled it out from underneath her pillow.

I laughed. "Why was it under your pillow? You know the Tooth Fairy only gives you money for teeth, not rubber bands."

"Ha-ha. Very funny. I put it there because I

didn't want Mom and Dad to see it when they kissed us good night."

"Okay, let's go do that first," I said, "and then when we come back upstairs, we'll draw Kenny's mustache."

"Okeydokey," said Kelly.

"Now remember, we have to be really quiet. We don't want to wake up Mom and Dad."

"What about that third stair?" asked Kelly.

"What about it?" I said.

"It creaks when you step on it."

"Oh yeah. I forgot about that."

"I know," said Kelly. "We could slide down the banister and skip that step altogether."

I smiled. "Good thinking, sis. Good thinking."

We tiptoed out of our room and down the hall to the stairs.

"Ready?" I whispered.

Kelly nodded.

I slid down the stair railing, and Kelly came down right after me.

As we started to walk across the living room, Kelly reached for the light switch. I grabbed her hand. "Are you crazy?" I whispered.

"What?" asked Kelly.

"We can't turn on the light."

"Then how are we supposed to see what we're doing?" asked Kelly.

"With this," I said, holding up a mini flashlight.

Kelly smiled.

I turned on the flashlight and led the way, as we tiptoed into the kitchen.

"Okay, I'll hold the flashlight," I said, "while you wrap the rubber band around the hose. That way you can see what you're doing."

There was no answer.

"Kelly? Kelly?"

Still no answer. I turned around to see Kelly with her head in the open refrigerator.

I tapped her on the shoulder. "Uh, what are you doing?"

"I figured since we were down here, I might as well have a little midnight snack," she said, pulling a pudding cup out of the refrigerator.

"Put that back," I said. "We have a job to do. We don't have time to eat!"

"Oh, all right," said Kelly, putting the pudding back in the refrigerator. "You're such a party pooper."

"Now come over here and put the rubber band on. I'll hold the flashlight, so you can see."

Kelly wrapped the rubber band once around the hose.

"I think you'd better wrap it around a few more times," I said. "We want to make sure it's on there good and tight."

"Okeydokey," said Kelly. She wrapped it around a few more times. "All set!"

"This is going to be so great!" I said. "When

54

Mom comes down to make breakfast, she's going to get sprayed right in the face!"

"It makes me laugh just thinking about it," said Kelly.

"Okay. Come on," I said. "We still have to draw the mustache on Kenny."

We tiptoed back to the stairs. Just as I was about to walk up, Kelly poked me.

"What?"

"Remember to skip the third stair from the top," she whispered.

I nodded my head and gave her a thumbs-up.

We slowly climbed the stairs, making sure to skip that step.

When we got to the top, I grabbed Kelly's hand, and we tiptoed into Kenny's room.

I pointed the flashlight into his crib.

"Oh, look at him. He looks so cute," Kelly whispered, "all snuggled up with his blankie."

"He's going to look even cuter with a mustache," I said, giggling.

I reached into his crib and drew the mustache
on his face.

Kelly started to giggle, too.

Kenny moved.

"Oh no! What if he wakes up?" said Kelly.

I put my finger to my lips to say *shhhhhh!*

Kenny made a couple of little noises.

We held our breath.

Then he pulled his blankie up around his chin and lay still again.

"Whew! That was a close one!" I whispered.

Kelly nodded. "Let's get out of here."

As we walked back into the hall, I accidentally stepped on one of Mike and Ike's dog toys that was lying on the floor.

It let out a loud *SQUEAK!*

When Mike and Ike heard the noise, they came running out of my parents' room, whimpering and running in circles.

"No! No! No! It's not playtime," I whispered. "It's time to go back to sleep."

Before I could grab the toy, Mike and Ike picked it up in their mouths and started to play tug-of-war. Every time they bit down, the toy made another loud *SQUEAK!*

Just then our mom came out of her room.

We froze.

"What's going on out here?" she asked us.

We just stared at her.

"Why are you two out of bed?

"Ummm . . . ummm," said Kelly.

"We had to go to the bathroom," I said.

"Both of you?" she asked. "At the same time?"

"Well, you know how twins are," I said. "We have to do everything together."

I don't know if our mom believed us, but she was too tired to argue. "You two need to get back into bed. It's a school night. You need your rest."

"Good night, Mom," we said. "See you in the morning."

"Good night, girls."

"That was a close one," Kelly whispered when we were back in our room.

"A little too close," I said.

"We'd better go to sleep," said Kelly. "We have a big day tomorrow."

"This is going to be the best April Fool's Day ever!" I said.

"You can say that again," said Kelly. "I can't wait!"

"Me, either, sis. Me, either!"

CHAPTER 6

The Big Day

On April Fool's Day morning, it was not our alarm clock that woke us up, but our mom's screams.

"AAAAAAHHHHHH! AAAAAHHHHHH!"

Kelly and I sat up in bed.

"She must have seen Kenny's mustache," said Kelly, laughing.

"Quick, grab the camera," I said. "We promised Jake we would take a picture."

Kelly grabbed the camera, and we raced out into the hall. Our mom was standing there, holding Kenny in her arms. Our dad was there, too.

"Say cheese!" said Kelly.

Kenny smiled a great big happy smile, and Kelly quickly took the picture.

"Girls, did you do this?" asked our dad.

We smiled.

"Why would you do such a thing to your brother?" asked our mom.

"April Fool's!" we said, laughing hysterically.

Our dad started laughing, too. "Good one, girls!"

"Bill, why are you laughing?" our mom asked him.

"Because it's funny. Kenny isn't hurt. He just has a little marker on his face."

"Don't worry, Mom," I said. "We made sure to use washable markers."

"Thank goodness," said our mom. "I wouldn't want to take him to story time at the library looking like this!"

"I'll wash him off," said our dad. "Why don't you go down and start breakfast?"

Our dad took Kenny into the bathroom, and Mom headed downstairs.

Kelly and I smiled at each other. "Here comes trick number two," Kelly said.

We listened carefully to our mom's footsteps. "I think she's in the kitchen now," I said.

"She'll be turning on the sink any second," said Kelly.

"Shhh!" I said. "Here we go. Three, two, one . . ."

"AAAAHHHH! AAAAHHHH!"

Kelly and I gave each other a high five.

Our dad came out of the bathroom with Kenny just in time to see our mom marching back up the stairs with her hair and face dripping wet.

Dad tried not to laugh, but he couldn't help himself. "Honey," he said, chuckling, "what happened to you?"

Kenny pointed to Mom and said, "Swim! Swim!"

"No, sweetie, mommy did not go for a swim,"

our mom told him. "Mommy got sprayed in the face by the sink hose when she turned on the water."

"April Fool's!" we said, and Kelly took another picture.

"At least you won't have to take a shower this morning," I said, giggling, "since you already took one in the kitchen sink."

"You two are Double Trouble," said our mom. "Why don't you go downstairs and wipe up the water off the kitchen floor while I go change into some dry clothes."

"Okeydokey," said Kelly.

"Okeydokey," said Kenny.

Kelly and I went downstairs and started mopping up the floor. "I think she got sprayed pretty good," said Kelly.

"I know," I said. "Look at all this water on the floor!"

"I wish I was down here to see it."

"Me, too!" I said.

"So far, so good," said Kelly. "The first two tricks worked perfectly."

"Now it's Dad's turn," I whispered.

Mom, Dad, and Kenny walked into the kitchen.

"All done, Mom," we said. "It's all wiped up."

"Thanks, girls. How about some breakfast?"

"Can we have eggs today?" asked Kelly.

"Eggs?" asked our mom. "I was about to make some oatmeal."

"But I really feel like eggs this morning."

"Eggs! Eggs!" said Kenny.

"See, Kenny wants eggs, too."

"Eggs! Eggs!" Kenny said again.

"Eggs sound good to me," said Dad.

"And just wait until you taste them," I whispered to Kelly.

"All right," said Mom. "If that's what everybody wants, then I'll make eggs."

She whipped up some scrambled eggs and put them on the table.

"Dad, why don't you serve yourself first," I said.

"Thanks, Kasey. Would you please pass me the salt?"

"Sure, Dad. No problem."

I gave him the salt shaker, and he shook some "salt" all over his eggs.

"Mmmmmmm, this looks delicious," said our dad. "I can't wait to taste it."

He put a big spoonful on his fork.

Kelly squeezed my leg under the table.

Dad took a big bite, started to chew, and then spit it out on his plate. "Phft, phft, phft!"

"Bill, what's wrong?" asked Mom.

"These eggs taste horrible!"

"I don't understand," she said. "I made them like I always do."

"Well, they taste *sweet*," said Dad.

"Sweet?"

"Yes, like they have sugar on them."

"Sugar? I don't put sugar in the eggs."

Just then Kelly and I burst out laughing.
"April Fool's, Dad!"

"Is this another one of your jokes?"

We nodded.

"We put sugar in the salt shaker," Kelly said.

"So when you went to put salt on your eggs

67

this morning, you actually sprinkled sugar all over them," I said.

"No wonder they tasted so sweet!" Dad said.

Our mom just shook her head. "You two are really something, you know that?"

We smiled. "We know."

"You two came up with some great tricks this year," said our dad.

"And we're not done yet," I whispered to Kelly.

Kenny started to bang his spoon on his tray. "Eggs! Eggs!" he said.

"Oh, you poor baby," said Mom. "We never gave you any eggs."

She put some eggs on Kenny's tray. "You girls need to eat your eggs now, too."

"It's getting late, and you're not even dressed yet," said our dad.

"The two of you take forever to pick out your clothes," said our mom.

"We actually have our outfits all picked out," said Kelly.

"Yep," I said. "We know exactly what we're going to wear today."

"Really?" asked our mom. "What a surprise."

"Oh, it's a surprise, all right," I whispered to Kelly. "It's a surprise!"

CHAPTER 7

The Twin Switcheroo

We got dressed in each other's clothes and dashed out of the house to catch the bus before our parents could see us.

We sat down in the seat across from Jake.

"So, how's it going so far?" Jake whispered.

"Awesome," I said.

"Really awesome," said Kelly.

"Did you take any pictures?"

"Yep," said Kelly. "Wait until you see

the picture of Kenny with a mustache. It's hilarious!"

"Ha, ha, ha, ha, ha!" Jake laughed. "I can just imagine it."

"And we also took a picture of our mom soaking wet from the sink hose," I said. "She looked like she had just gotten out of the shower."

"All of your ideas were great!" said Kelly.

"We still have two of the best ones left," I said.

"So did you guys remember to bring the green food coloring?" asked Jake.

"Yes, I have it right in here," I said, patting the pocket of my backpack.

"And we came up with a plan for you to distract Madison, so Kasey and I can put the drops in," said Kelly.

"When it's snack time, you'll knock her furry pink jacket on the floor when you get out your snack," I said. "She'll freak out and run to pick it up. That's when we'll put the drops in."

"Great plan!" said Jake. "She's so crazy about that jacket."

"I don't get it," said Kelly. "It's just a jacket."

"By the way," Jake whispered. "You guys look great. No one is going to realize that you did the big switcheroo."

"Thanks," we said.

The bus pulled up to school, and we got ready to get off. I reached for my yellow backpack.

Kelly poked me. "What are you doing?" she whispered.

"What do you mean, what am I doing? I'm getting my backpack."

"That's not your backpack today. Remember?"

I laughed. "Oh yeah. Today my favorite color is green, not yellow."

"And you like peanut-butter cookies, not chocolate-chip," said Kelly.

"But they're so gross," I said.

"No, they're not. They're delicious," said Kelly.

"Come on, guys. You're holding up the line," said Jake.

We all got off the bus and walked to our room.

Mr. Lopez looked at Kelly and said, "Good morning, Kasey."

Kelly didn't answer. I poked her.

"Oh, good morning, Mr. Lopez," she said.

Then he looked at me and said, "Good morning, Kelly."

"Morning, Mr. Lopez," I said.

We walked over to our cubbies to put our stuff away. Then I walked over to my desk to sit down, forgetting that I should be sitting at Kelly's desk today.

"Hey, Kelly, why are you sitting at Kasey's desk?" asked our friend Jasmine.

"What?" I said.

Kelly walked over. "Hey, sis, get out of my seat."

I jumped up. "This is going to be harder than I thought," I whispered to Kelly.

"I know what you mean," Kelly whispered back.

"You'd better watch out, Kasey," said Jasmine. "I think your sister was about to play an April Fool's Day trick on you."

"I almost forgot it was April Fool's Day," said Jake.

"Me, too," said Kelly.

"Not me," said Madison. "I remembered it was April Fool's Day. I even played a trick on my mom this morning."

"You did?" said Jake.

"Yes," said Madison. "I put on my red shoes instead of my pink ones. Isn't that a great trick?"

"That's not a trick," said Jake. "That's just lame."

"No, it's not," said Madison. "My mom thought it was hilarious."

"Then your mom's a weirdo."

"No, she's not."

"Yes, she is."

"Okay, enough, you two," said Mr. Lopez. He turned to Kelly. "It's time to get started. Kasey, would you please lead us in the Pledge of Allegiance?"

Again, Kelly just sat there. I kicked her in the leg and motioned with my hand for her to get up.

"I'd be happy to, Mr. Lopez," she said. Kelly led the class in the Pledge, and then we started our morning math lesson.

"I would like to do a little review before the test today," said Mr. Lopez. "I have a problem written on the board. See if you can solve it."

We all took a few minutes to try the problem at our desks.

I poked Kelly. "Hey," I whispered. "I don't know how to do this problem, but I just know that Mr. Lopez is going to call on me because he thinks I'm you, and you are a math genius."

Kelly scribbled the answer on a scrap of paper and secretly passed it to me.

"Okay, I think everyone is done," said Mr. Lopez. "Who would like to come up and show us how they solved the problem?"

"Oh, me, me, me, me, me!" squealed Madison. "I just know I have the right answer."

"I'm looking for someone who isn't calling out," said Mr. Lopez.

Andy, the shyest kid in the whole class, was sitting quietly.

"Madison, do you see how Andy is not calling out?"

Madison glared at Andy. "Andy, would you

like to come up and show us how you solved
the problem?"

Andy shook his head. He was always too shy
to stand up in front of the class.

Mr. Lopez then looked at me. "Okay, then.
How about you, Kelly?"

"I knew it," I whispered to myself. "I just
knew it."

"Why don't you come up to the board and show us how you figured it out?"

I really didn't want to, but if I didn't go, then everyone would figure out that we had switched places. I stood up. "Sure thing, Mr. Lopez," I said.

I glanced back at Kelly. "You can do this," she whispered.

I took one last look at the scrap of paper and went up to the board. To my surprise, I was able to solve the problem.

"Nice work, Kelly," said Mr. Lopez. "I knew you could do it."

I walked back to my seat.

"Nice work, sis," said Kelly.

"Yeah," said Jake. "No one suspects a thing."

CHAPTER 8

The Biggest Surprise of All

We did some more review for the math test, and then it was time for snack.

"I'm so excited for snack today," said Madison. "My mom packed me a special surprise. I can't wait to see what it is."

"Oh, you're going to have a surprise, all right," Jake whispered to me.

I giggled. "Remember the plan. When you go to get your snack, you have to knock her pink, fluffy jacket on the ground. When she runs to pick it up, Kelly and I will put the food coloring in her milk."

Jake gave me a thumbs-up.

Madison started to unpack her snack. The girl's favorite color is pink, so everything she has is pink: pink lunch box, pink thermos, even pink napkin.

Madison clapped her hands. "Oh, look, everyone," she said, holding up a cupcake. "My mom made me a rainbow cupcake with pink frosting and pink sprinkles!"

"Whoop-de-doo," said Jake.

Madison unscrewed the cap to her thermos and looked inside. "Good thing my mom packed me milk. Milk goes perfectly with cupcakes."

"Yes, good thing," I whispered to Kelly.

Jake stuck his finger into the frosting on Madison's cupcake.

"Get your dirty little hands off my cupcake,"

said Madison. "Go get your own snack, Jake the Snake."

Jake licked the frosting off his finger and walked over to the cubbies to get his snack. He knocked Madison's jacket on the floor just like we had planned.

"Uh, Madison, excuse me," said Andy. "I think your jacket is on the floor."

"No, it's not," said Madison. "I hung it up this morning."

"Take a look," said Andy, pointing to the floor.

Madison stood up. "Oh no! My pink, fluffy jacket! How did it get on the floor? It's going to get dirty!"

She turned and pointed her finger at Jake. "*You* just knocked it on the floor."

"No, I didn't," said Jake.

"Yes, you did. Now go pick it up!"

"No," said Jake. "You can't boss me around. It's your jacket. You go pick it up."

"Get ready," I whispered to Kelly.

Madison glared at Jake and stomped over to the cubbies to pick up her jacket.

"Now!" said Jake.

I snuck the green food coloring out of my lunch box while Kelly grabbed Madison's open thermos and put it on my desk.

"Hurry up!" said Kelly.

"I'm hurrying," I said. I took the top off the food coloring and dropped a few drops into the milk.

"She's coming back now," said Jake.

Kelly quickly put the thermos back on Madison's desk.

Madison sat back down. "Lucky for you, Jake Brown, my jacket didn't get dirty. If it had, you would have been in big trouble."

"Oh, I'm so scared," said Jake.

"Just leave me alone, so I can enjoy my cupcake," said Madison.

She took a big bite.

Andy giggled.

"What's so funny?" said Madison.

Andy stopped giggling.

"I'll tell you what's so funny," said Jasmine, laughing. "You've got a pink frosting mustache."

"I guess it's the day for mustaches," I whispered to Kelly.

Madison quickly grabbed her napkin and wiped her face. "Now, for some delicious milk to wash it down."

"Here we go," whispered Jake.

Madison put her straw in her thermos and started to sip.

Andy stared at her.

"What are you staring at?" said Madison.

"Your . . . your . . . your . . . ," Andy stammered.

"My what?" said Madison.

"Your milk is green," said Andy.

"Ewwwww," said Jasmine. "You're drinking rotten milk!"

Madison looked down at her thermos and then started to run around the room screaming, "Eeeewwwwwww! Eeeewwwwwww! My milk is green! My milk is green! I'm drinking rotten milk!" As she was running, she bumped into her desk and the thermos fell over. Green milk began to spill onto the floor.

Mr. Lopez stepped in front of her and held out his hands. "Calm down, Madison. What's the problem?"

"My milk is green! Look at it! My milk is green! I'm being poisoned!"

We all were laughing hysterically.

"Why are you all laughing? I'm going to get sick!"

"You're not going to get sick," I said.

"How do you know?" said Madison.

"April Fool's!" Kelly, Jake, and I said.

"What?" said Madison.

"What?" said Mr. Lopez.

"April Fool's!" I said again. "You're not drinking rotten milk. We put food coloring in your milk to make it look green."

"Good one," said Jasmine.

"Thanks," said Jake, smiling.

"All right," said Mr. Lopez. "That was quite a trick." Then he pointed to Kelly and said, "Kasey, would you please go get a sponge so we can get this mess cleaned up?"

"Okeydokey," said Kelly, and she started to walk toward the sink.

"Wait a minute," said Mr. Lopez. "What did you say?"

"Okeydokey," Kelly repeated.

"'Okeydokey'?" said Mr. Lopez. "You never say 'okeydokey,' Kasey."

Just then Kelly realized her mistake.

"Only Kelly says 'okeydokey,'" said Mr. Lopez.

The two of us just stood there, frozen.

"Something fishy is going on here," said Mr. Lopez. "Come over here, girls."

We walked over to him.

He pointed to Kelly. "Let me see your leg."

Kelly pulled her pants up to the knee, revealing a Band-Aid.

"I knew it! I knew it!" said Mr. Lopez. "You're Kelly," he said, pointing to Kelly, "and you're Kasey," he said, pointing to me. "Kelly fell off her bike a few days ago and scraped her knee. She's been wearing a Band-Aid ever since."

"April Fool's!" Kelly and I said together.

"Wow! You girls really had me going! That is one of the best April Fool's Day tricks I have ever seen!"

"Thanks!" we said. "It was actually Jake's idea."

"Good one, Jake," said Mr. Lopez.

Jake smiled. "Give me a high five, guys," he said.

Kelly reached up her hand. "Okeydokey!" she said, and we all laughed.

DOUBLE TROUBLE FUN PAGE

Can you spot five differences between Kasey and Kelly?

Kasey

(and Mike)

Kelly

(and Ike)

Have you read all about Freddy?

Don't miss any of Freddy's
funny adventures!

These twins are

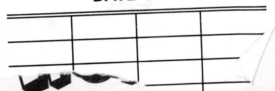

Double Trouble
Show & Tell
by ABBY KLEIN

illustrated by
JOHN McKINLEY

SCHOLASTIC

Double Trouble
April Fool's Surprise
by ABBY KLEIN

illustrated by
JOHN McKINLEY

SCHOLASTIC